Hi! I'm Pencil!

written by
Deanne Hritz

illustrations by
Wendell Washer

WestBow Press books may be ordered through booksellers or by contacting:

WestBow Press
A Division of Thomas Nelson & Zondervan
1663 Liberty Drive
Bloomington, IN 47403
www.westbowpress.com
844-714-3454

Interior Image Credit: Wendell Washer

Scripture taken from the New King James Version®. Copyright © 1982 by Thomas Nelson. Used by permission. All rights reserved.

ISBN: 978-1-6642-2485-8 (sclf)
ISBN: 978-1-6642-3723-0 (sc)
ISBN: 978-1-6642-2486-5 (e)

Library of Congress Control Number: 2021903605

Printed in the United States of America.

WestBow Press rev. date: 09/23/2021

WestBow
PRESS®
A DIVISION OF THOMAS NELSON
& ZONDERVAN

Thank you to my granddaughter, Katherine, for her challenging me to write this book, and to my wonderful husband whose selfless involvement made it possible. Without both of them, Pencil would not have had a chance to make his mark on the world.

---Deanne Hritz

Hi! I'm Pencil!
These are my colorful friends.

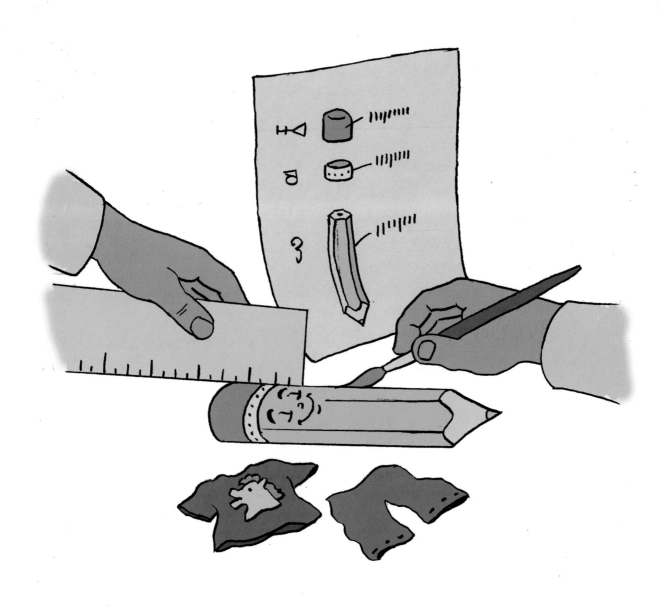

We are created and designed to
do many things.

Although the world is full of other
really cool pencils in many
different colors, ...

...I am here for a purpose.

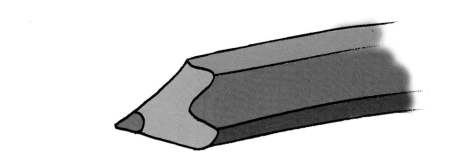

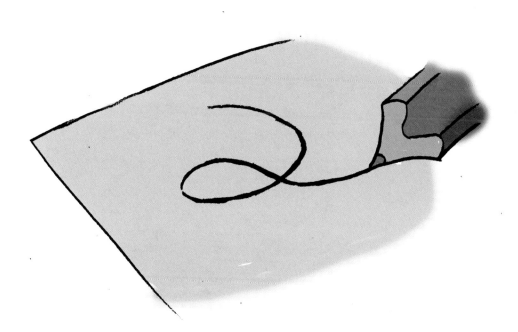

I have a point.
I make marks with it.

I am unique because I will do
things no other pencil will do.

My marks are my own.

My designer knows that pencils make mistakes.

Oops!

I thank you that I have a soft eraser.

Rub – rub – rub.

Now that's better!

Making mistakes is part of who I am.

love
joy
peace

I can write about good things
that make people happy.

Or I could put down words that are
harmful or just bad.

Oh! And I may be able to draw
beautiful pictures ...

... of God's creatures and people, too.

When I am in the hand of my designer,
I can do awesome things!

But sometimes I may find myself
in the hand of someone else, ...

... and then mistakes happen, like this.

I could write things that make me
ashamed.

Then it is good to use my soft eraser.
Rub - rub - rub.

Yet sometimes it leaves a dirty smudge ...

... if it is used a lot.

It is good to be a pencil
in the hand of my designer.

I want to do wonderful things.

I want my designer to be happy
with whom He has made.

Just look at what we did.

I think we made Him smile.

I like that!

What will my tomorrows be like?

Only my designer knows!

For God so loved the world
that He gave His only begotten Son,
that whoever believes in Him
should not perish
but have everlasting life.
John 3:16